Michael H

Red

A Crayon's Story

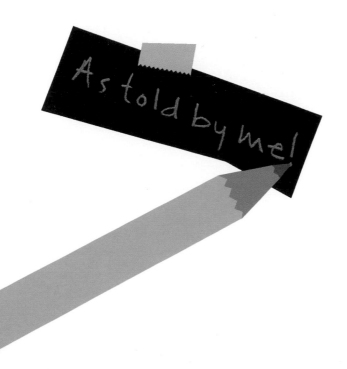

As told by me!

SCHOLASTIC INC.

He was red

But he wasn't
very good at it.

Oh dear.

His teacher thought
he needed more practice

I'll draw
a red
strawberry,
then you
draw a red
strawberry.

You can
do this.
Really!

But he couldn't, really.

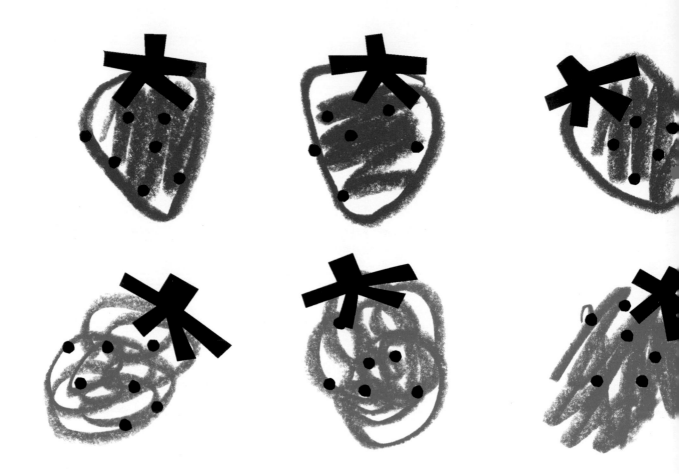

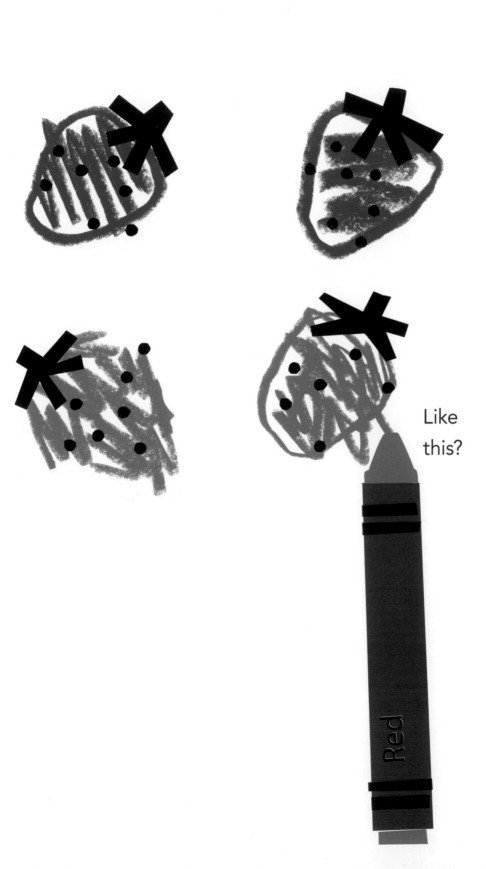

Like
this?

Oh my!
Let's try
again.

His mother thought he needed
to mix with other colors.

Why don't
you two
go out
and draw
a nice,
round
orange.

A really
big one.

A really
orange
one!

But they made
a big greenish one.

Yuck!

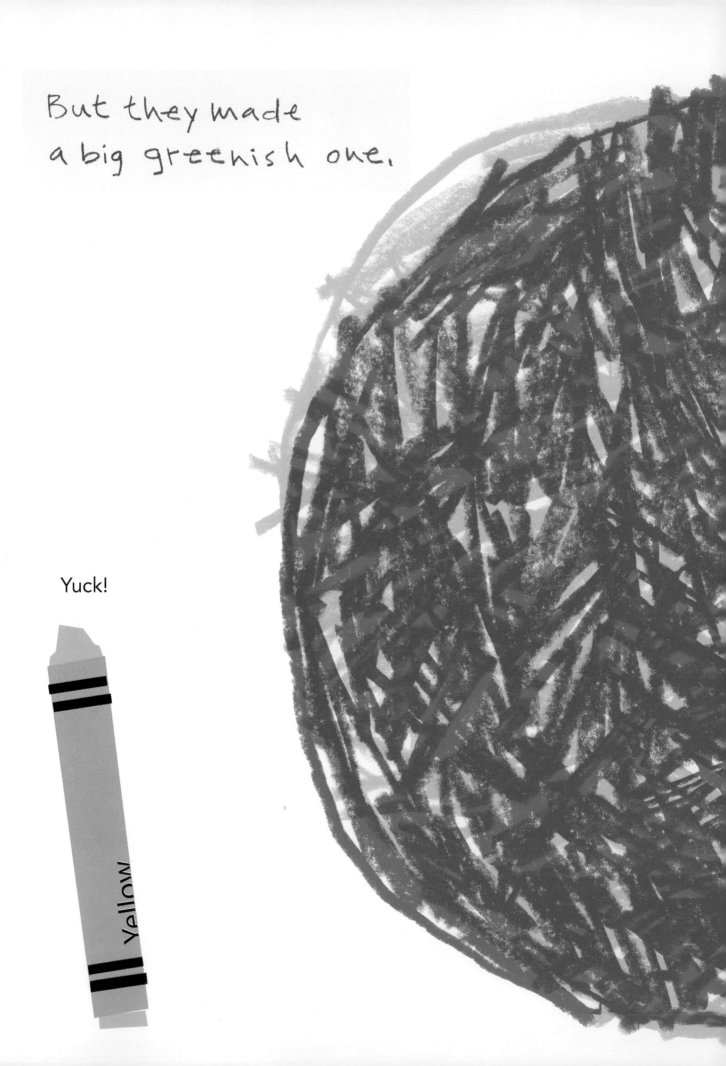

Oops.

His grandparents thought
he wasn't warm enough

Your class is making self-portraits for parents' night. Wear this warm red scarf.

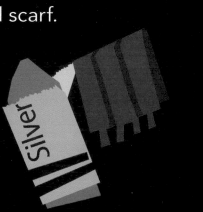

Red

Nice! It's so you!

But it so wasn't.

Red

oranje

Grey

Olive

Silver

Gray

Oh,
dear
me.

Everyone seemed to have
something to say

Sometimes
I wonder
if he's really
red at all.

Don't
be silly.
It says
red on
his label.

He came
that way
from the
factory.

Frankly,
I don't
think
he's very
bright.

Amber

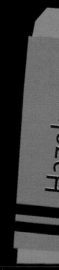

Hazelnut

Cocoa Bean

Fuchsia

Well,
I think
he's lazy.

Right!
He's got
to press
harder.

Really
apply
himself!

Give
him
time.
He'll
catch
on.

Of
course
he
will.

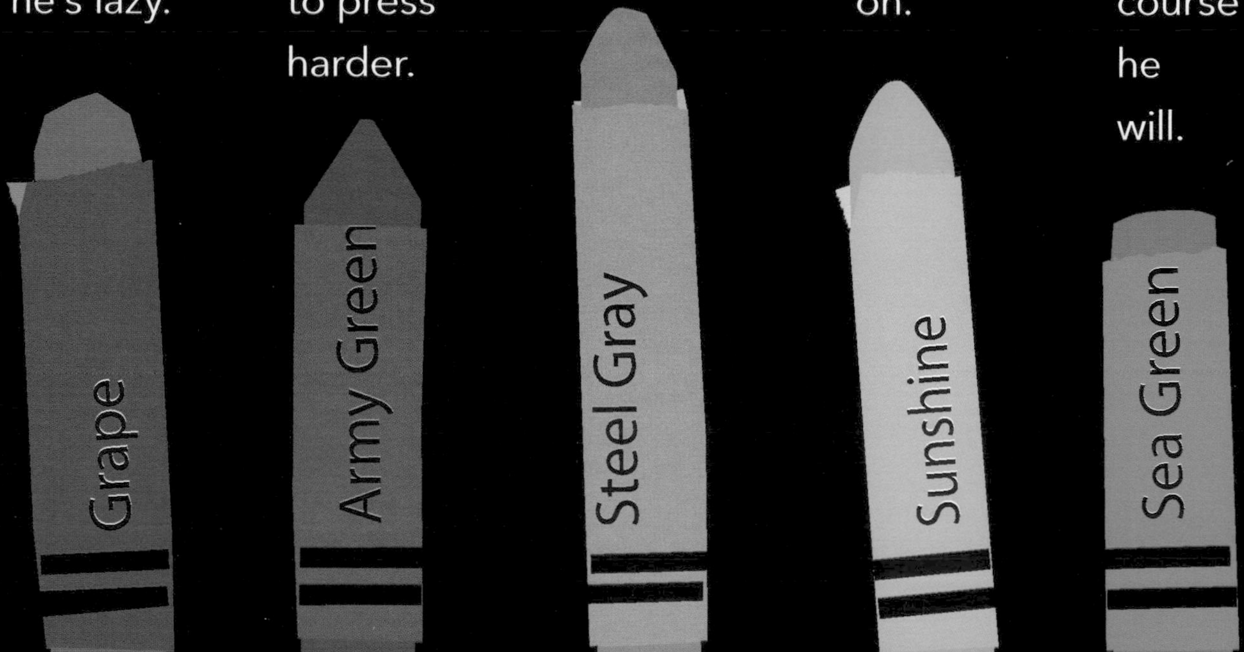

Grape

Army Green

Steel Gray

Sunshine

Sea Green

But he didn't catch on.

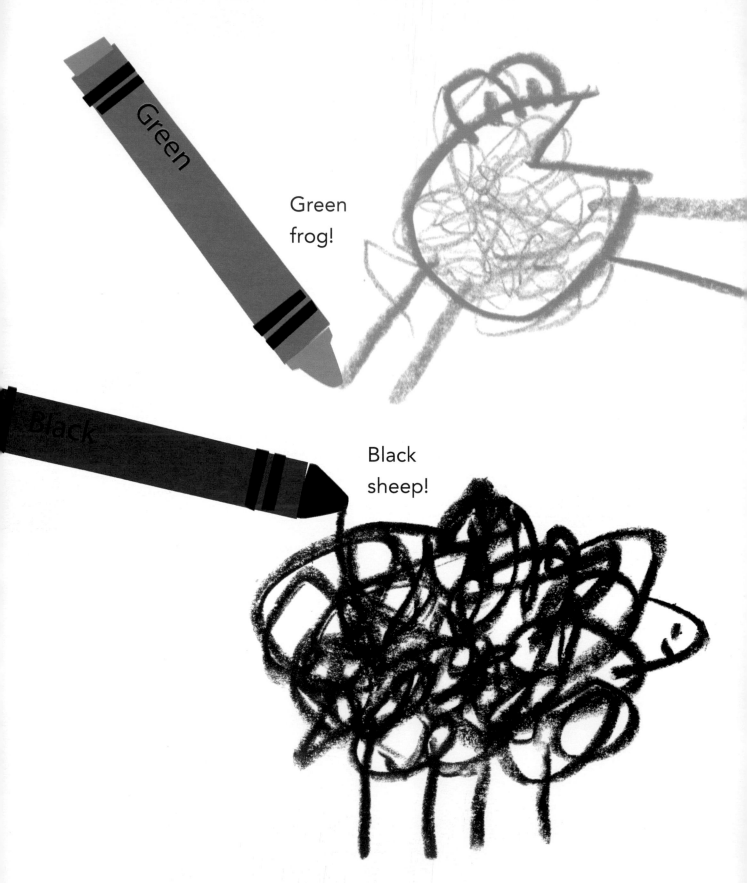

Green
frog!

Black
sheep!

Brown
cow!

Red . . .
aaack!

All the art supplies
wanted to help.

The masking tape thought
he was broken inside.

This will
help hold you
together.

The scissors thought his label was too tight.

One
snip
should
do it.

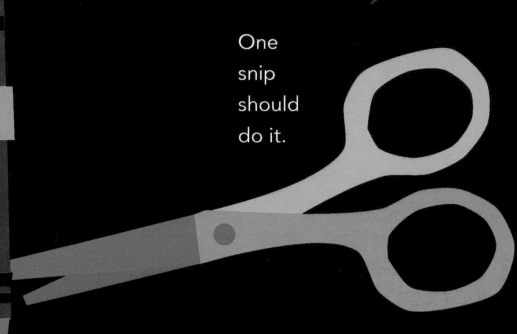

I thought he wasn't sharp enough.

Stay
still,
now.

But even with all our help

and all his hard work,

he just couldn't get the hang of it.

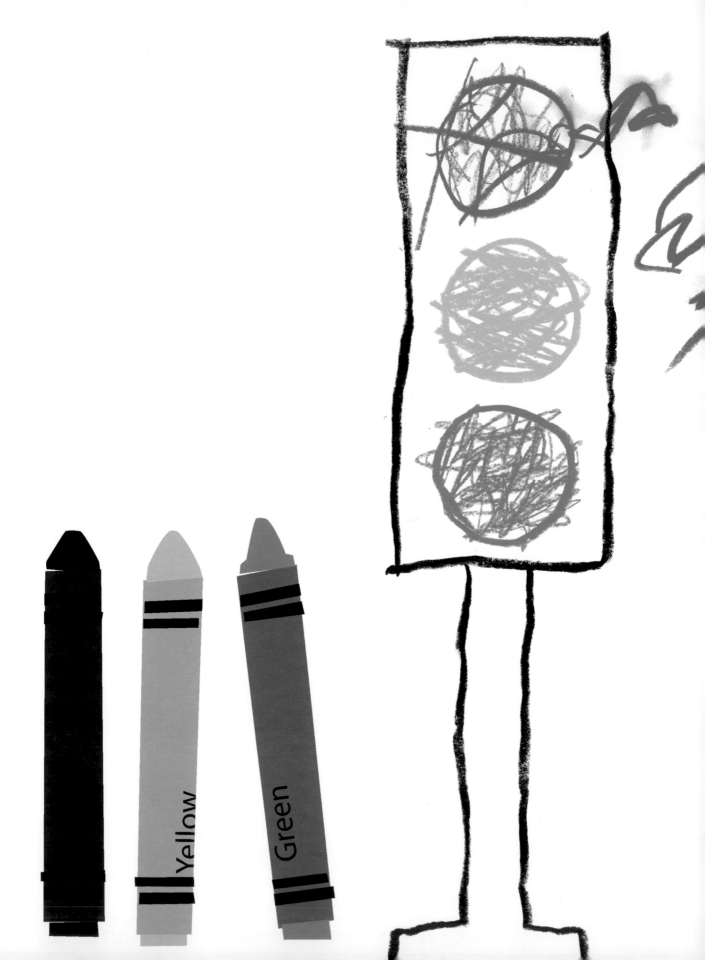

One day, he met a new friend,

Will
you
make
a blue
ocean
for my
boat?

I can't.
I'm red.

Will
you
try?

So he did.

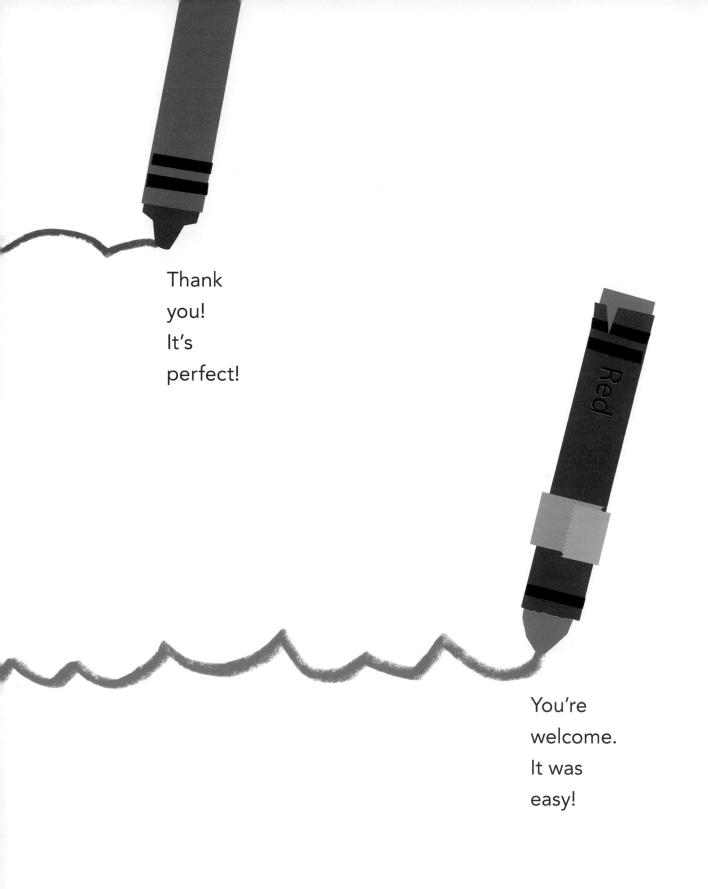

Thank
you!
It's
perfect!

You're
welcome.
It was
easy!

And he didn't stop there.

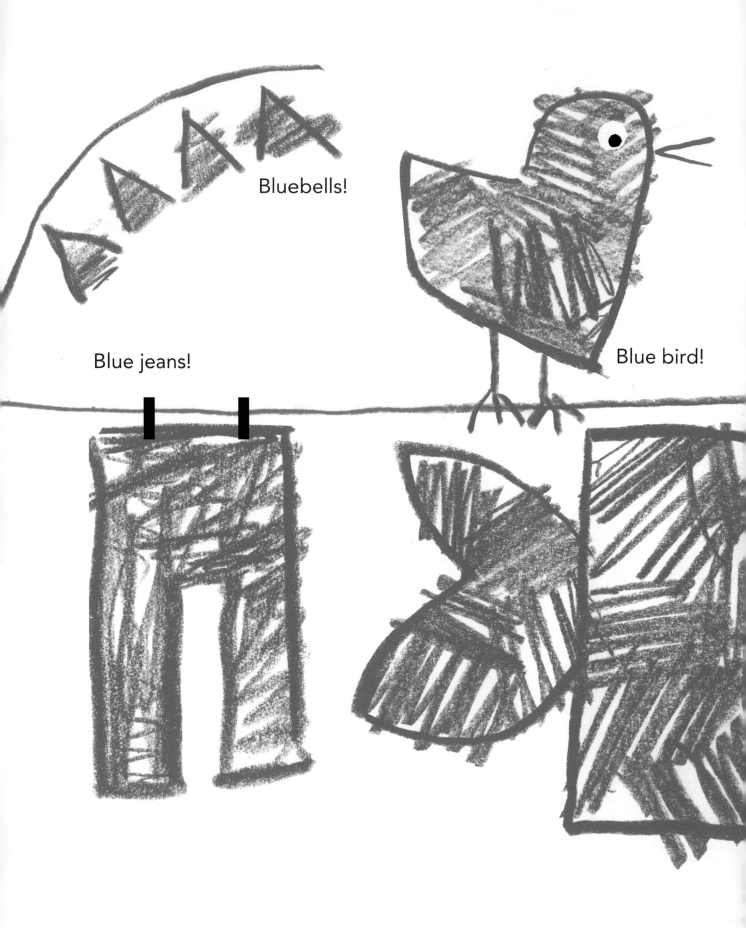

Bluebells!

Blue bird!

Blue jeans!

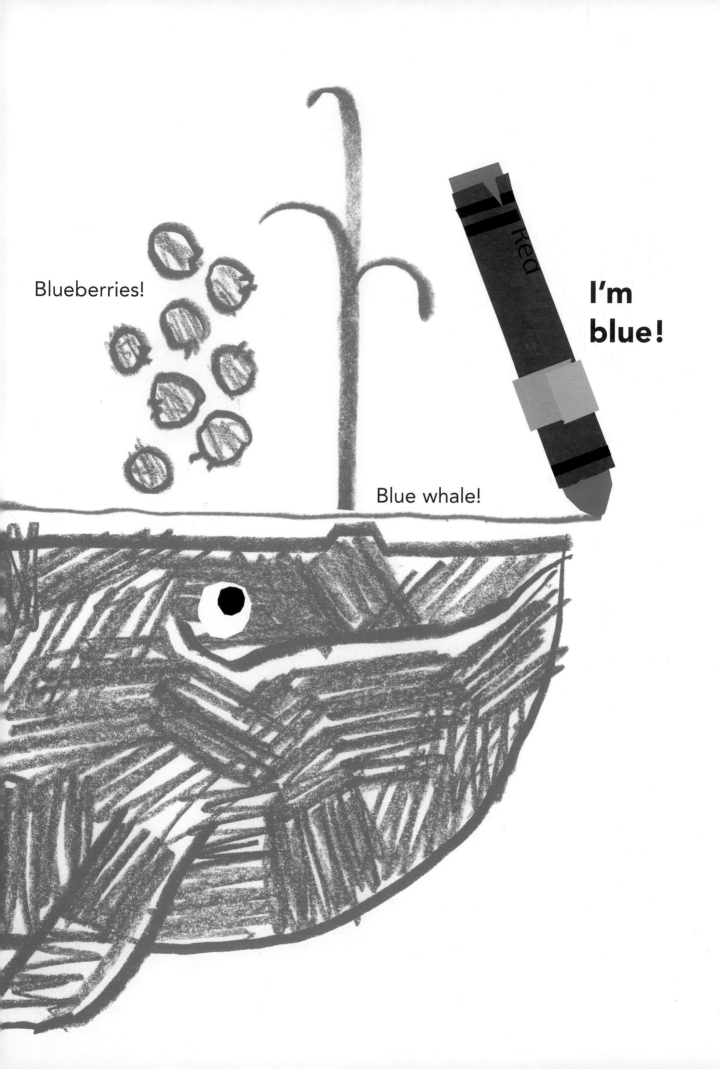

Blueberries!

Blue whale!

I'm blue!

He was ~~red~~ blue.
And everyone was talking.

His
blue
ocean
really
lifted
me.

All
of
his
work
makes
me
happy.

My
son
is
brilliant!

Who
could
have
known
he was
blue?

I
always
said
he
was
blue.

It
was
obvious!

Olive

Amber

Hazelnut

Cocoa Bean

Berry

Sea Green

His
blue
strawberries
are my
favorites.

I'm
going
to make
a green
lizard
with him.
A really
big
one.

He's
really
reaching
for
the
sky.

He's
so
intense.

I hear
he's
working
on a
huge
new
project.

Brown

Apple Gre

Yellow

Gra\

Scarlet

For
Debra

ISBN 978-1-338-10651-0

Copyright © 2015 by
Michael Hall. All rights
reserved. Published by
Scholastic Inc.,
557 Broadway,
New York, NY 10012,
by arrangement with
Greenwillow Books, an
imprint of HarperCollins
Publishers. SCHOLASTIC
and associated logos
are trademarks and/or
registered trademarks of
Scholastic Inc.

12 11 10 9
19 20 21

Printed in the U.S.A.   169

First Scholastic printing,
September 2016

The art consists of
digitally combined and
colored crayon drawings
and cut paper.

The text type is
Avenir Light.